Jeffrey Lee,
Future Fireman

**BY MARCIA LEONARD
PICTURES BY ANN IOSA**

Silver Press

For Keith Mackler.
—M.L.

To my special son, Michael.
—A.I.

Library of Congress Cataloging-in-Publication Data
Leonard, Marcia.
    Jeffrey Lee, future fireman / by Marcia Leonard;
pictures by Ann Iosa.
      p. cm.—(How did that happen?)
    Summary: Jeffrey takes a tour of the firehouse with his
class and dreams of the time when he is grown up and can be a
fire fighter too. At various points in the text the reader is asked
to explain what is happening.
    [1. Fire departments—Fiction. 2. Fire fighters—Fiction.
3. Occupations—Fiction. 4. Literary recreations.]
I. Iosa, Ann, ill. II. Title. III. Series: Leonard, Marcia.
How did that happen?
PZ7.L548Je   1990
[E]—dc20   90-31299
ISBN 0-671-70403-6 (lib. bdg.)   CIP
ISBN 0-671-70407-9 (pbk.)   AC

Produced by Small Packages, Inc.
Text copyright © 1990 Small Packages, Inc.

Illustrations copyright © 1990 Small Packages, Inc.
and Ann Iosa

Published by Silver Press, a division of
Silver Burdett Press, Inc.
Simon & Schuster, Inc.
Prentice Hall Bldg., Englewood Cliffs, NJ 07632.

Printed in the United States of America.

10 9 8 7 6 5 4 3 2 1

More than anything, Jeffrey Lee wanted to be a fireman.
So when his class visited the fire station, he made sure
that he was at the front of the group.

Captain Keith showed them around. "This is the dispatch office," he said. "When people report fires, their phone calls come in here. Then the dispatcher signals the fire fighters." Jeffrey studied the computers and the phone system. Suddenly there was a loud ringing noise!

How do you think that happened?

Did the teacher
ring a bell to dismiss
the class for recess?

Did Santa ring a bell
to celebrate Christmas?

Did the dispatcher
ring the bell that alerts
the fire fighters?

Or did the butler
ring a bell to call
everyone to dinner?

"When the dispatcher rings the alarm bell, the
fire fighters come running," said Captain Keith.
"It doesn't matter *what* they're doing!"

"They might be sitting at the table eating a meal,"
he went on, showing the class the kitchen.

"Or they might be fast asleep in their beds," he said,
taking the children upstairs to the bunk room.
"But wherever they are, they come on the double."
Then as Jeffrey watched, Captain Keith stepped past
the lockers—and disappeared!

Now how did that happen?

Did Captain Keith
squeeze into a locker?

Did he slide down
the fire pole?

Did he get
snatched up by aliens?

Or did he melt into
a puddle on the floor?

"Sliding down the pole is the quickest way for fire fighters
to reach their trucks," Captain Keith called from below.
"But you kids will have to take the stairs."
"Okay," Jeffrey called back. "But when *I'm* a fireman,
I'll slide down the pole, too!"

"Fire fighters are always in a hurry," Captain Keith said
when the class joined him downstairs. "That's why we keep
our boots by the fire engine and the doors open." He smiled
at Jeffrey. "Now who would like to try on some of the gear?"

"Me, me!" cried Jeffrey, jumping up and down.
So Captain Keith helped him put on a long, heavy
fireman's jacket and a big pair of boots. "You need
one more thing to make the outfit complete," he said.
"What's that?" asked Jeffrey. Then everything went black.

How did that happen?

Did the sun
decide to set early?

Did Jeffrey decide
to play blind man's bluff?

Did the fire hat
cover his eyes?

Or did a monkey unscrew
the light bulbs?

"I guess the hat's a little big," said Captain Keith.
"Yes," said Jeffrey, pushing it back from his eyes.
"But when *I'm* a fireman, it will fit just right."

Captain Keith showed the class the air tank and face mask
that fire fighters wear so they don't breathe in smoke.
Then he took them around to see the hook and ladder truck,
the pumper, the rescue van, and the snorkle truck.

Jeffrey noticed an empty parking space in the station. "Some of our fire fighters are out on a call," explained Captain Keith. "But it was a small fire, so the truck should be back soon." Just then the station door rolled open. There was a beeping sound, and lights started flashing.

How did that happen?

Did Captain Keith
turn on a giant video game?

Did an airplane
come in for a landing?

Did a robot
roll in through the door?

Or did the returning fire truck
back into the station?

Jeffrey and his classmates watched as the truck backed into
the station and the fire fighters put away all their gear.

Then Captain Keith said, "I want to introduce you to
our mascot Blaze! He lives right here in the station,
and he's friends with all the fire fighters."
"When *I'm* a fireman, he'll be my friend, too," said Jeffrey.

Just then Blaze reached out and gave Jeffrey a big lick.
Captain Keith laughed. "I don't think you'll have to wait until
you're a fireman," he said. "Blaze is your friend right now!"